KID SQUAD

SAVES THE WORLD

The Madness of Captain Cyclops

by John Perritano   Illustrated by Mike Laughead

Calico

An Imprint of Magic Wagon
www.abdopublishing.com

www.abdopublishing.com

Published by Magic Wagon, a division of ABDO, PO Box 398166, Minneapolis, Minnesota 55439. Copyright © 2015 by Abdo Consulting Group, Inc. International copyrights reserved in all countries. No part of this book may be reproduced in any form without written permission from the publisher. Calico™ is a trademark and logo of Magic Wagon.

Printed in the United States of America, North Mankato, Minnesota.
052014
092014

THIS BOOK CONTAINS RECYCLED MATERIALS

Written by John Perritano
Illustrated by Mike Laughead
Edited by Rochelle Baltzer and Megan M. Gunderson
Cover and interior design by Candice Keimig

Library of Congress Cataloging-in-Publication Data

Perritano, John, author.
  The madness of Captain Cyclops / by John Perritano ; illustrated by Mike Laughead.
       pages cm. -- (Kid Squad saves the world)
  Summary: When the testing of a nuclear-powered invisibility device goes awry, Captain Rudolph Von Dorn is transformed into the evil Captain Cyclops, blowing up ships and islands at will--and the Kid Squad, with the help of Von Dorn's daughter Jenny, is called upon to reverse the effects of the accident and save the world.
  ISBN 978-1-62402-040-7
1. Heroes--Juvenile fiction. 2. Military weapons--Accidents--Juvenile fiction. 3. Submarines (Ships)--Juvenile fiction. 4. Scientists--Juvenile fiction. 5. Inventions--Juvenile fiction. 6. Adventure stories. [1. Heroes--Fiction. 2. Invisibility--Fiction. 3. Submarines (Ships)--Fiction. 4. Scientists--Fiction. 5. Inventions--Fiction. 6. Adventure and adventurers--Fiction.]
I. Laughead, Mike, illustrator. II. Title.
  PZ7.P43415Mad 2015
  813.6--dc23
              2014005819

Table of Contents

Chapter 1
Foggy Fall Night

"It's a wonderful night, isn't it, sir?"

"Yes it is, Barkley. It certainly is. You can smell the salt in the air and feel the wind skipping off the sound."

Rudolph Von Dorn loved nights like this. He could hear the water of Connecticut's Thames River flowing gently into Long Island Sound. For centuries, captains, sailors, whalers, merchants, and fishermen called the old port city of New London home.

Von Dorn had arrived in New London ten years earlier with seawater in his veins. His father had served in the Vietnam War. His grandfather was a ship mechanic during World War II.

Unlike his relatives, though, Von Dorn took a different path to the sea. After graduating from the US Naval Academy, Von Dorn taught for a time at the Naval War College in Newport, Rhode Island.

Von Dorn, still in the US Navy, was now the lead researcher at Electrocycle Industries, helping the navy develop its finest submarines. Although his twelve-year-old daughter lived on another coast, Von Dorn's home was the Thames River. That's where Electrocycle Industries had a research facility and the navy had its most prized submarine base.

On this fall night, all was silent aboard the bridge of the USS *Harpoon* as fog crawled up the river.

"The sea makes a man free," Von Dorn said to Barkley. "That's why I love it out here. I'm glad we picked tonight to test the Invisashield. Is everyone aboard?"

"They are, sir," Barkley responded. "Just waiting for your orders."

"Very good," Von Dorn acknowledged. "Go below and make sure everything is in order. I'd like to stay up here for a moment or two."

"Take as long as you like, sir," Barkley said. "I'll see to it that everyone is set to go. All ninety-eight crew members are working tonight. No one wanted to miss the test."

"Excellent," Von Dorn said. "Admiral Williams has his carrier strike group out there waiting for us. Keep your fingers crossed and hope the Invisashield works."

Ah yes, the Invisashield. It had taken six years of research, work, more research, and more work. Tonight would be the final test of the Invisashield, a name Von Dorn had given the Electromagnetic Invisibility Cloaking Device that he had helped develop and had just finished installing in the *Harpoon*. If everything went according to plan, the device would wrap the submarine in a high-energy field and make it invisible.

The device was revolutionary. It had the ability to change the face of naval warfare. Imagine if a ship, especially one carrying nuclear missiles as the *Harpoon* did, could sail the world's oceans unseen by human eyes, satellite, or radar. No one would dare threaten the United States again.

Von Dorn thought about these things as he looked into the night sky. He watched the stars flicker in the infinite blackness.

He stood silently, gazing down the river, the lights of the New London submarine base reflecting gently on the water. Von Dorn could see his breath dance on the cool air. He became wistful thinking about his daughter, Jenny, who was living with her mother in California.

I sure miss her, Von Dorn thought as he rubbed his tearful eyes. *I haven't seen her in over a year.*

Maybe she can spend next summer out here. She'd love New England. Hopefully she'll want to stay here with me for a while.

Von Dorn and his crew were about to learn that dreams, no matter how big or small, are as elusive as the blowing wind.

¤

"Everybody is at their stations, captain," Barkley shouted as Von Dorn climbed down into the submarine.

"Very good, lieutenant," Von Dorn answered. "Let's cast off the lines."

Within moments, the USS *Harpoon* slid gently away from its moorings. It traveled slowly to the mouth of the Thames and into Long Island Sound. Within a half hour, the submarine swam into the open Atlantic. The plan called for the *Harpoon* to engage Admiral Williams's carrier group about 150 miles out.

The *Harpoon* was the world's most sophisticated and most powerful nuclear submarine. It carried dozens of cruise missiles that could soar through air faster than sound and hit targets 1,200 miles away. Its ultra-sensitive sonar could detect vessels moving some 3,000 miles away. Its nuclear reactor was powerful enough to allow the *Harpoon* to cruise nonstop for twenty-five years.

Von Dorn's nuclear-driven Invisashield could render the 7,400-ton ship undetectable indefinitely. With all its high-tech systems, the *Harpoon* could travel an astounding 600 miles a day under the water or 1,000 miles a day at the surface.

"We're in open water now, captain," Barkley yelled across the control room. "We'll soon be running parallel with Block Island."

"Radar and sonar both confirm that the carrier strike group is 150 miles south-southwest," reported Sully, the sonar technician.

"Very good," Von Dorn said. "Let's dive. We'll make sure Williams sees us before we engage the Invisashield. Then we'll take each of his ships one at a time. Of course, this is just a game, ladies and gentlemen. But it's an important game."

Chapter 2
Those Poor Souls

"There she is, sir. There's the *Harpoon*. She's about 100 miles north of us and diving quickly."

"Keep an eye on it," ordered Admiral Williams. "Make sure you don't break that uplink with the satellites. If we lose the connection, we'll lose our eyes for sure."

Admiral Cyrus Williams knew the importance of the simulated battle. It had been his idea to create the Invisashield in the first place. He knew what it could do, although his sailors and pilots did not. Williams had to defend against something that he wouldn't be able to see or hear.

"It's gone, sir," the sonar operator said in utter confusion. "It was there one moment, and now it's not. I'm checking the uplink with the satellites, but all seems to be in order."

This is it, Williams thought. *The* Harpoon *is cloaked. Let's see how it swims.*

"Sound general quarters," shouted the admiral. "All hands to battle stations. Launch the planes. It's time to go to war."

¤

"Full speed ahead, Barkley," Von Dorn commanded. "On my order, we will fully engage the Invisashield. Williams won't know what hit him when I pull up beside him and slap that round head of his."

"Aye, aye, captain," Barkley responded. "Full speed ahead."

The Invisashield was working wonderfully at 25 percent power. Von Dorn surmised that the *Harpoon* was off everyone's sonar and radar screens. He only hoped the satellites flying in Earth's orbit were equally as blind. Increasing to 100 percent power, the *Harpoon* could surface and still be invisible. That was the beauty of the Invisashield.

The Electromagnetic Invisibility Cloaking Device was Von Dorn's most ambitious invention. He hoped it would be the one that would make him famous. *Perhaps I'll even get a medal for this. I wish Jenny was aboard*, he thought. *She's never seen her old man in action.*

Racing furiously underwater, the *Harpoon* neared the carrier strike group. The group consisted of one aircraft carrier, one cruiser, two destroyers, seventy aircraft, and 7,500 men and women.

"Bogeys at three o'clock, captain!" shouted Sully. "They're fifty miles out and closing fast."

"Admiral Williams launched his planes. All right, let's see what the *Harpoon* can do when the Invisashield is fully engaged. Lieutenant, will you do the honor?"

"Aye, aye, captain," Barkley yelled with uncontrollable glee. "I'm fully engaging the Invisashield . . . *now*."

With that, Barkley adjusted a few controls and the Invisashield purred like a kitten. Theoretically, no one—not even a passing shark—could see the *Harpoon*.

"Surface," Von Dorn ordered. "I want to park this baby under the admiral's nose."

"Aye, aye, captain," Barkley responded, and began slowly bringing the *Harpoon* to the surface.

The cloaking device wrapped the submarine in a protective electromagnetic blanket. Despite the enormous energy it took to keep the ship invisible, the *Harpoon* didn't glow under the dark water or generate any heat. It was a scientific miracle.

It's working . . . it's working, Von Dorn thought as the *Harpoon* slid around the back of Williams's carrier group. Everything was going according to plan, until the unthinkable happened.

Before the *Harpoon* could surface, warning sirens rang out as the Invisashield malfunctioned. The automatic override should have shut down the device's nuclear power supply, but it had blown a circuit. It was not responding as the Invisashield began to overheat.

The alarm caught everyone by surprise.

"What's going on down there?" Von Dorn barked into the *Harpoon*'s intercom, hoping that Stephens, who was in charge of the Invisashield room, could take care of the problem.

"Captain, the device is malfunctioning. The radiation gauge is off the chart. I can't shut down the device, sir. It's going to explode! We have two minutes."

"Can you manually override it?" Von Dorn asked in a panic. "Pull its plug?"

"Negative. She's not responding to anything we can do."

Von Dorn, in crisis mode, put down the intercom for a second and thought. His next orders were crisp and final.

He told Stephens to shut off the Invisashield room from the rest of the submarine. A series of airtight, radiation-proof, blast-proof doors would lock. He hoped the doors would be enough to contain the radiation in the stern of the ship.

Stephens and those poor souls will be trapped. They'll be microwaved, fried to bits, Von Dorn thought. *Such is the life we choose.*

"Surface, surface!" Von Dorn then yelled to Barkley. "Blow the hatches when we hit the top. Prepare to abandon ship."

Before Barkley could respond, the Electromagnetic Invisibility Cloaking Device spewed a torrent of radiation. Amazingly, there was no fire, nor explosion. Still, a bright light flashed as superheated air whooshed down the *Harpoon*'s corridors. Finally, the *Harpoon* broke the surface. Its nose rocketed out of the water like a breaching whale.

The radiation did not damage the interior of the ship, nor the Invisashield itself. Yet it harmed the crew in the most grotesque and amazing ways. They were no longer people it seemed . . . but alien-like creatures, especially Von Dorn, whose two eyes melded into one on his forehead. He looked like a mythical Cyclops of ancient Greece.

Admiral Williams saw the bright flash of light illuminate the horizon behind his carrier group. An hour later, the carrier group vanished.

The navy's official report later claimed that the carrier group was lost in a freak Atlantic storm that disappeared as fast as it came. Only a few people knew the truth, however. Williams and his crew were the first victims of the USS *Harpoon* and its now maniacal commander— Captain Cyclops.

Chapter 3
Stars of the Show

The highlight of the year at Copernicus Middle School was the *Fall Follies*. If you believed the flyers taped to all the walls and classroom doors, the event was a "Star-Studded Extravaganza Guaranteed to Keep Your Feet Stompin' and Your Heart Pumpin'."

Everyone looked forward to the *Follies*, especially the students and teachers who sang a song or performed a skit. This year was especially notable because Tank and the rest of the football team—Coach Ryan included—decided to perform a rib-splitting rendition of Rodgers and Hammerstein's classic "I'm Gonna Wash That Man Right Outa My Hair."

The kids might not know anything about the showstopper from the musical *South Pacific*, but the song was destined to be the most special of performances. This was because all the players and Coach Ryan were planning to wear hula skirts when singing. Tickets to the show sold out quickly after everyone found that out.

While Tank, Coach Ryan, and their football friends were slated to be the comedic hits of the *Follies*, it was Gadget, Samantha Longstreet, and Dorothy West who ultimately stole the show. The trio had been practicing the popular aria "Habanera" from the opera *Carmen*. Samantha spent weeks singing the song in Italian while Gadget and Dorothy accompanied her on their cellos.

DADA DA DA dada da da dada da dadadadada da da DADA DA DA, the melody went. Gadget and Dorothy played their sixth-grade cello hearts out. Gadget liked the opera about a beautiful gypsy woman named Carmen and Don Jose, the Spanish army officer who falls in love with her.

"What sixth-grader loves opera?" Tank teased Gadget after learning his best friend was going to perform during the *Follies*. "Seriously, Gad old boy, you're one twisted pretzel. Why don't you take that oversized fiddle of yours and play something less boring?"

"A cello is not a fiddle, you dork burger," Gadget shot back. "Besides, Samantha has a wonderful voice. We're going to bring down the house."

"Yeah, on our heads," Tank replied.

Bring down the house is exactly what Gadget, Samantha, and Dorothy did. Samantha hit all the right notes, and Gadget and Dorothy played as they had never played before. They got the biggest ovation out of anyone.

"Oh my, that was so beautiful," Athena gushed, giving Gadget, Samantha, and Dorothy each a big hug. "I mean, who knew that opera was so awesome. I already added your song to my playlist."

"You were great," said Pi. "Everyone stood on their feet and cheered. Did you hear Craig Lumpersickle whistle? He's the biggest bully in school, but even he stood up and applauded. Bravo, Gadget, Sam, and Dorothy. Bravo."

Even Tank was amazed at how wonderful the aria sounded. Still in his hula skirt and coconut bikini top, Tank walked over to his best bud and slapped him on the shoulder.

"Couldn't have done it better myself, Gad old boy. The three of you had Mrs. Huxley in tears. She never cries. She's a statue."

Just then, Pi reached into her pocket as her cell phone buzzed. There was an emergency. Dr. I. N. Stein and Colonel Ulysses T. Bragg called on the Kid Squad to meet at their headquarters —a series of rooms under the basement of Pi's house.

"Looks like the after party will have to wait," Pi said. "Let's get out of here."

¤

Dr. Stein sat in his laboratory deep in the Amazon rain forest. Colonel Bragg flew in a stealth plane high above the Atlantic Ocean. Both had been monitoring the test of the *Harpoon*'s cloaking device when things went horribly wrong.

They had had direct communication links with both Von Dorn and Admiral Williams. When things went silent, Dr. Stein and Bragg knew something was up.

Satellite photos showed that the carrier group had disappeared. Where the *Harpoon* was, no one knew. A search of the area by hundreds of planes and ships revealed nothing. That's when Bragg and Stein called the Kid Squad into action. The men appeared at Kid Squad headquarters in a holophone transmission.

The holophone was a cool communication device that Gadget had helped invent. Although people might be thousands of miles away, it allowed them to appear in the same room together. They could talk to one another as if they were sitting across the breakfast table.

Bragg explained that the US Navy had ships and planes looking for the *Harpoon*. As Dr. Stein so aptly put it, "they will never find zee *Harpoon* because it is invisible and can stay that way for a long, long time."

"How do you know the *Harpoon* wasn't destroyed?" Pi asked.

"That's a good question," Bragg said. "We don't believe the sub was damaged, nor the cloaking device. If so, we'd have seen the mess it made.

"It is our opinion that something malfunctioned aboard the *Harpoon* relating to the device," he continued. "What that was, we don't know yet. Frankly it doesn't matter at this point. But we believe that whatever happened caused Von Dorn and his crew to destroy the carrier group. They must have gone mad!"

"If the carrier group was destroyed, wouldn't you have found some debris floating in the water?" Gadget asked. "There are a lot of ships in a carrier group. They just don't disappear when blown to pieces."

"That is a good point, my boy," Dr. Stein said. "It is zee question that has puzzled me also. Unlike Colonel Bragg, I do not believe that zee carrier group is *kaput*. I've been doing some calculations and I think Von Dorn, how you say, *figured out*, yes, figured out, how to use zee electromagnetic energy from zee cloaking device to create a ray of some kind that makes zee other ships invisible."

"Really?" Tank said.

"Dr. Stein thinks the carrier group is still out there, invisible, unable to contact us, or we them," Bragg said. "We can't see it. They can't see us. I'm skeptical, but it's possible. They're sort of like in suspended animation. They're there, but they don't know they're there."

"As if they were in, how you say, *another dimension*, yes, another dimension," Dr. Stein said.

"What do you want us to do?" Pi asked.

"The cloaking device is the most sophisticated bunch of wires and circuits the navy has," Bragg said. "I need you guys to find the *Harpoon*. It's imperative. The ship has nuclear missiles, and if I think what has happened has happened, Von Dorn has gone off his rocker . . . he's become a scrambled egg . . . a French fried potato. If someone in that condition has access to nuclear weapons, I don't have to tell you what might happen."

The members of the Kid Squad looked at one another.

"It's invisible, right?" Athena said. "So how are we supposed to see it?"

Chapter 4
Terror on the Ocean

"Mommy, Mommy, is that a whale?"

The excited seven-year-old pointed across the railing of the *Ivy Sue,* the best whale watching boat anywhere in New Jersey. The child's mother squinted in the sunlight. She raised a hand to shield her eyes from the glare off the water.

"I don't see anything, honey," the child's mother said. "There's nothing out there."

But there was something out there, at least for a brief moment. The child had seen it, as did a few of the other passengers. To the child it looked like a big whale. To the adults, it looked like a sea monster. It was there one moment, and gone the next.

As the *Ivy Sue* cut across the water, a bright flash of light lit up the already bright sky. In a second, the *Ivy Sue* was gone, as were its whale watchers. When the boat didn't return to her dock, the US Coast Guard launched a massive search.

They found nothing.

¤

Seventy miles south of the *Ivy Sue*, Sasha and David Manual were celebrating their fiftieth wedding anniversary aboard their sailboat the *Golden Years*. When they didn't show up for their family anniversary dinner later that night, the coast guard searched the area.

As with the *Ivy Sue*, the coast guard found nothing.

Later that week, a Brazilian container ship disappeared. Two days later, four charter fishing boats out of Myrtle Beach, South Carolina, never returned home.

The Atlantic was quickly becoming a cemetery of ships.

It didn't take long for the news media to grab hold of the story. "Sea of Lost Ships," one headline declared. "Graveyard of the Dead?" said another. "Where Are They?" one website wanted to know.

"Why are these ships disappearing without a trace?" a local TV news reporter asked as she stood beside a fleet of fishing boats, her helmet of blonde hair weighed down with massive amounts of hair spray. "No one really knows. Some suspect strong currents dragged each of these vessels to the bottom of the ocean. Others claim aliens are responsible.

"Whatever the reason, the boats in this fleet behind me, and others like them, stay tied to their docks. Some witnesses have told authorities that they saw a large whale-like creature, possibly a sea monster, in the distance moments before an unusually bright light illuminated the sky. No one is hazarding a guess as to what these witnesses might have seen. One thing is certain, however—this part of the Atlantic Ocean is now ghostly quiet."

¤

"What are your orders, captain?" barked the *Harpoon*'s second-in-command, Lieutenant Barkley. Although the officer who answered to that name a few days before was not at all the officer who was now second-in-command of the *Harpoon*.

The malfunction of the cloaking device had turned the *Harpoon* into a ship of lost souls. All crew members, Barkley included, had undergone a massive physical and mental transformation.

Physically, the accident disfigured each crew member to the point of utter grotesqueness. They looked like badly-drawn cartoon characters.

Barkley, who now wanted people to call him Lieutenant Spider, was one of the most hideous. Half his face was gone, its skin hanging loose like melted plastic. His right hand was missing. In its place, he had duct-taped a fork from the *Harpoon*'s galley. A huge hump had grown on his back, and he now walked with a bad limp.

Mentally, the accident caused each crew member to go mad in his or her own way. Perhaps the most insane was Rudolph Von Dorn himself, once the top of his class at the Naval Academy and the star quarterback in high school. The man with a daughter named Jenny was now a tyrant of the sea.

The radiation blast fueled rage in Von Dorn, whose crew now called him Captain Cyclops. He sought to use his intelligence and the *Harpoon* to wreak havoc wherever he could. He fancied himself a modern-day Captain Nemo in a heavily armed *Nautilus*.

Crew members blindly and gladly followed Cyclops. His mission was their mission. No questions asked. No order was too crazy to obey.

"Keep our course south-southeast," Captain Cyclops answered, his voice now rough and thick. "We're going to continue testing this new ray I developed and work out its kinks. Right now, we're using the Invisible Ray to turn ships invisible. But I want to be able to destroy them. I also want to fire these nuclear missiles. I'm thinking of turning Washington DC into a crater. Maybe some other cities, too."

"The navy is going to be looking for us, captain, that's for sure," Lieutenant Spider said.

"You are right, my lad, but they won't be able to find us," the captain said. "We have enough fuel and food to stay afloat for nearly a year. We can travel underwater as long as we want, except when we use the Invisible Ray. As

long as the Invisashield is working correctly—
Stephens has seen to that—they won't be able
to see us. We're going to have a grand time. A
grand time."

"Captain, I spot a ship to starboard," yelled Sully the sonar technician. Like Spider's, Sully's mutated face had seen better days.

Unlike other submarines, the *Harpoon* did not need a periscope to see what was happening on the surface. Instead, Sully raised two masts to the surface, each carrying thermal and low-light cameras. Once the masts broke the surface, Captain Cyclops had a 360-degree picture of what was around the *Harpoon*.

The captain looked at the visuals and licked his puss-yellow lips. *I'll be*, he thought. *It is. It is.*

"We can put a torpedo into its bow if we don't want to use the Invisible Ray," said Spider. He secretly wished to blow a ship to smithereens instead of making it disappear.

"Negative!" Cyclops yelled. "Prepare a boarding party. That vessel is the *Iron Eagle*."

"That's President Novak's personal yacht," Spider said.

"The one and only," Cyclops said. "The president is not aboard, but his daughter and wife are. Before we left New London, I read that they were vacationing on the Outer Banks. Now they're 400 yards away."

"What nice shipmates they will make," Spider said, seeing the evil gleam radiate from the captain's eye.

"Indeed, lieutenant, indeed," the captain said. "There are four heavily armed navy patrol boats around her. I'll let you have your fun with those. You know what to do. Make it fast."

"Aye, aye, captain," Spider acknowledged as a gleeful smile cracked across his mangled face. "Surface on my order and fire the ray at the navy boats. Do not hit the *Iron Eagle*."

Chapter 5
Novak's Demands

The Amulator was getting a workout as never before. Each member of the Kid Squad used the world's most powerful device in an attempt to locate Captain Cyclops and the *Harpoon*.

As usual, the kids worked as a team. Pi and Gadget each used the Amulator to create two transportspheres. These bubble-like vehicles could fly into outer space or plumb the depths of the ocean.

Pi flew high above the Atlantic. She hoped the transportsphere's ultrasensitive sensors and computers could spot the *Harpoon* or the missing ships.

Gadget took his transportsphere underwater. "Zee only way to catch zee fish," Dr. Stein had

37

told Gadget, "is to get in zee water with them." With that, Gadget plotted the points of all the mysterious ship disappearances and slowly trolled for the *Harpoon*.

Athena and her cat, D-Day, coordinated the entire search from Kid Squad headquarters. Actually, Athena coordinated the search. D-Day just curled up in a little white ball and slept on top of one of the computer monitors. He loved its warmth.

Meanwhile, Tank searched for Jenny, Von Dorn's daughter. Bragg believed Jenny could help them if they ever found Von Dorn and his submarine. Tank started his search online, hoping to find some trace of the girl.

As for Bragg and Dr. Stein, they had the toughest assignment of all. They had to explain to the president of the United States how the *Harpoon* had become a rogue ship and what they were doing about it.

Although it was a bright, sunny autumn day in Washington DC, the mood at the White House was becoming increasingly dark. President Novak was mad, very mad.

The president had opposed the cloaking device from the beginning. He didn't believe it was worth all the money and effort. But the military minds at the Pentagon, including Bragg, had pushed him to approve the project. The president let Bragg know the cloaking device was a huge blunder, "one that may cost you your job, colonel," the president reminded him.

The situation had taken on a more dire tone when the coast guard found the *Iron Eagle* floating sixty miles off Cape Hatteras, North Carolina. The president's wife, his daughter, and the yacht's crew were missing. So were the four navy vessels whose job it was to protect the First Family.

"Bragg, is it really possible that Von Dorn is responsible for all these ship disappearances? He and that cloaking device?" the president asked.

"It seems likely, sir," Bragg said.

"Do you think the ships that have suddenly vanished from the planet are destroyed, including the navy boats that were protecting my family?"

"*Nein*, no, Mr. President," Dr. Stein interrupted. "I believe that all zee ships are still there, somewhere. But we cannot see them, nor can they see us."

"What about the *Iron Eagle*?" the president demanded.

"Zee *Iron Eagle* is different," Dr. Stein said. "Zee *Iron Eagle* was left intact because your wife and daughter are, how you say, *hostages*, yes, hostages aboard zee *Harpoon*. Von Dorn didn't make zee boat disappear because he wanted to get your attention."

The president, sitting at his desk, put his head in his hands in exhaustion and frustration, not to mention anger. He stopped for a moment and regained his composure. "He certainly got that," he said.

"However, Mr. President," Dr. Stein continued, "I believe that zee *Harpoon* will no longer be turning ships invisible."

"What do you mean, doctor?" the president asked.

"It is my belief that Von Dorn will turn zee ray he is using to make zee ships invisible into a weapon of, how you say, *mass destruction*, yes, mass destruction. I have done some calculation. I believe it is possible to use zee energy from zee cloaking device and turn the Invisashield into a weapon."

"Well that's just great. What are you and your group doing to find the *Harpoon,* Bragg?" the president blared.

"We're doing every dog-blasted thing we can do, sir," Bragg said to the commander in chief. "Everyone in the Special Projects Division is working overtime. Even the Kid Squad, sir. Every square inch of the Atlantic is being combed for clues. We'll find this traitor if it's the last thing we do, sir."

"I've heard enough!"

Vice President Jerome Hershey rose from his seat in the corner of the Oval Office. He adjusted the knot on his red tie and pulled down the lapels on his suit jacket. He walked slowly toward the president's desk.

The vice president had no trouble speaking his mind, even in front of his boss. Gruff, sometimes surly, and twenty years older than the president, Hershey wanted to be commander in chief. But the man now occupying the White House had beat him in the primaries three years before. *My time will come*, Hershey thought. *Soon.*

Hershey shook his head in disbelief.

"Mr. President, with all due respect, Colonel Bragg and Dr. Stein, not to mention Admiral Williams, bungled this whole cloaking device project from the beginning. I wouldn't trust them to clean up a litter box. They're in over their heads with this mess, sir.

"I suggest we use General Marsh's group. They have no-nonsense ways of solving problems. Her team has moved into position. She's in direct communication with the International Space Station, which is scanning the ocean as we speak. Once we find the *Harpoon*, we will blast it out of the water with everything we can muster."

The president got up from his chair and walked over to the window behind his desk. Outside, the sun was blazing down on the city.

"I see what you mean, Jerome. Duly noted," the president said, nodding. He then turned around and looked his vice president square in the eye. "At this moment, I have full confidence in Colonel Bragg's team, especially the Kid Squad. They have never failed us before. I suspect they'll come through this time. At least for the time being, we'll let them handle this situation."

"It could get worse, Mr. President," Hershey shot back. "You know that. And if it does, you will get the blame. You know that, too. Frankly, once again with all due respect, sir, Von Dorn has supposedly taken your family hostage. I believe that might be clouding your judgment."

"Once again, duly noted," the president said abruptly. "I suspect I will get the blame for anything that happens. Still, I won't tell the press that *you* pushed the navy to develop the Electromagnetic Invisibility Cloaking Device. You want to be frank? Okay, let's be frank, shall we? I won't put the interests of my family in front of the interests of the nation. Is that clear, Mr. Vice President?"

The vice president stood silent. He wasn't sure the president could keep that promise.

"Is that clear, Mr. Vice President?"

"Crystal clear, sir."

"Bragg . . . Stein . . . show some results or I'll have your heads," the president demanded. "Understand?"

"Yes, Mr. President," Colonel Bragg and Dr. Stein said at the same time.

The vice president was right, though. It got worse, much worse.

Chapter 6

Gadget the Traitor

Once there was a dot of an island just off the coast of Bermuda.

Then there wasn't.

Gadget saw the tiny spec disappear in a blaze of light. "Holy guacamole!" he shouted as the blast rocked the transportsphere.

No one lived on the island. Captain Cyclops thought it would be a great place to test what he called the Destructo Beam. The weapon obliterated the island.

As Dr. Stein feared, the captain had used his evil genius to turn the Invisible Ray into a beam of deadly light. Next he used the Destructo Beam on seven abandoned beach houses in Florida. He blew them away in a breeze of hot light.

It was only a matter of time before Cyclops turned the Destructo Beam against the world's cities. Websites, newspapers, and TV stations published the images of the shattered homes and the remnants of the island. A panic spread along the East Coast.

"It's obvious that something is causing all this destruction," a TV reporter blared into a microphone, "but military officials refuse to comment on the situation."

The report then showed Colonel Bragg walking out of the White House into a throng of reporters with cameras and microphones held high.

"Colonel, what's going on in the Atlantic?" one reporter shouted.

"Colonel, what is the military doing to stop the attacks?" another cried.

"Colonel, is it true we're under alien attack?"

Bragg said nothing and drove off in a long, black limousine.

Meanwhile, Gadget used the Amulator's access pad he wore around his wrist to scan the sea. He was certain the *Harpoon* was close. He had unexpectedly caught a glimpse of what looked like a large whale before the island off Bermuda vanished.

After an hour or so, the device detected a faint trace of radioactivity off the coast of North Carolina. Gadget programmed the transportsphere to follow the trail.

"Transportsphere 2 to HQ. . . . Transportsphere 2 to HQ," Gadget radioed, using the transportsphere's visorscreen to talk to Athena at Kid Squad headquarters. "Come in. . . . Come in."

"This is HQ," Athena answered. "How's it going, Gad?"

"I'm following a trail of radioactivity. It's just a dusting of particles. I'm not sure what it is, but I'll bet you dollars to donuts it's the *Harpoon*."

"Roger that, Transportsphere 2. I'll relay that info to Pi. I'll have her lock on to your position and begin scanning. I'll alert Colonel Bragg and Dr. Stein, too."

"Roger that, Athena. There's one other thing. I can't say for sure, but I believe the *Harpoon* has to drop its invisibility cloak before firing its ray."

"Roger that," said Athena. "I'll pass it along. Be safe, Gad. I don't want anything to happen to you. Neither does D-Day."

"Gotcha. And thanks. Transportsphere 2 signing off."

At that moment, D-Day did something curious. The minute Gadget uttered his last syllable, the cat jumped onto Athena's lap.

"*Meowww*," the cat whined. Then he swiped Athena's nose with his paw.

"Bad kitty!" Athena yelled, shooing D-Day off her lap. "Why did you do that?"

D-Day ran to the visorscreen where Gadget's image had just been. He started meowing furiously as he pawed the screen.

D-Day knew Gadget was in trouble.

¤

Gadget followed the stream of radioactive particles for several hours along the coasts of Delaware and New Jersey. The radioactivity, like an unseen snake, took a slight right turn, passing New York City. It then moved along the south shore of Long Island. It slunk west into Long Island Sound toward Connecticut.

Then the trail vanished.

Gadget checked the Amulator to make sure it was still working. It was. He made sure the transportsphere's sensors were working, too.

"Holy guacamole!" he yelled. "It's gone."

Gadget was just about to tell Athena the news when the transportsphere shook. It suddenly descended into a vortex of spinning water.

Gadget thought he was in a blender. The transportsphere spun wildly out of control, contorting the skin on Gadget's face—the result of gravity's pull. His glasses flew off his head. Gadget struggled to look out the window. The water was a gray blur.

He then passed out.

When the boy awoke, he found himself face-to-face with a hideous one-eyed creature. Gadget was a bit fuzzy. He had no recollection of where he was or how he got there.

"What do we have here?" Captain Cyclops said as Gadget blinked the dizziness out of his eyes. "It looks like the young man who's been following my ship for nearly a day now. Those missile blasts made short work of that contraption you were in."

Gadget shook the fuzziness out of his head and stared at the one-eyed ghoul. He took off his glasses to rub his eyes.

"Who are you?" Gadget whispered. "What do you want?"

"I should be asking you those questions," Cyclops shot back. "And what is this?"

The captain held Gadget's Amulator access pad. He studied it carefully. "Ah, yes, I've heard about this device. I thought it was a fable, an urban legend. Yet now I have one of its controls in my hand. It controls a device called the Amulator, yes?"

Gadget remained silent.

"Stop me if I'm wrong, son, but the Amulator is the most powerful device in the world, isn't it? I've heard of its existence. I did have top secret clearance once. It can transport people into space. It can destroy cities if need be, can it not?"

Gadget said nothing.

"Yes, yes it can," Cyclops continued. "It's a time machine and a weapon rolled into one, among many other things. I thought the Invisashield was genius, but this takes the proverbial cake. In the right hands, it can make a person invincible. A god, almost."

Terror filled Gadget's eyes.

"Yes, I can see I am right. I figured Bragg would try to find me. You're part of that squad of children he has, aren't you? Yes, I've heard rumors about you and your friends. Like to save the world, do you? Well not this time, lad. Let me introduce myself. My name is Captain Cyclops. I am in command of the *Harpoon* and its mutated crew. What is your name?"

Gadget did not answer. He stared into the Captain's one eye, realizing the man had once been Von Dorn.

"Ah, yes, you're a good soldier, aren't you? Never give the enemy any information. I commend you. No matter, we'll get to know each other soon enough. You must be smart if you're with Bragg's crew. I was monitoring your transmissions to your headquarters. You're very bright. I can use a man like you."

"I'll never join your crew," Gadget yelled.

"Oh, you're already part of the *Harpoon*. Welcome aboard. Just do me a favor, if you don't mind. Look deep into my eye."

Gadget did not want to look into his revolting eye, but something inside him couldn't resist. It was horrible, yet alluring. Gadget soon fell into a hypnotic trance and obeyed the commands of the demented captain.

Hours later, Gadget found himself at the helm of a second nuclear submarine containing a backup cloaking device. Gadget had helped Captain Cyclops steal the *Harpoon*'s sister ship, the *Hurricane*, from the New London base. Now both vessels cruised under the sea, invisible to prying eyes.

Each ship was armed with a Destructo Beam, several atomic warheads, and deadly cruise missiles. More important, Cyclops now had control of the Amulator itself. He would use it and the president's family to terrorize the planet.

Chapter 7

Cyclops Goes Berserk

Tank rang the doorbell. It had taken him two days to track down Jenny Von Dorn in San Diego, California. Now he was about to tell her a story that would send shivers down her spine.

The door opened and out stepped a woman with a broom in her hand. She was older, about sixty. Tank guessed she was the housekeeper.

"Hello, may I help you?" she politely asked Tank.

"Um, I'm looking for Jenny," Tank responded in a soft voice.

"May I say who's calling?" the woman asked.

"My name is Joshua Barton, but everyone calls me Tank."

"And what might I ask is this regarding, Mr. Barton?"

Tank could feel his face get flushed. He was as nervous as a raccoon in the middle of the day. *Jeez Louise, lady, I didn't come here to get asked a thousand questions*, he thought. *I just want to tell Jenny that her father has gone mad and has kidnapped the president's wife and daughter*.

"Um . . . Um . . . I'm a friend of her dad's."

"Captain Von Dorn?" the woman asked.

"Yes, ma'am," Tank said.

The woman silently closed the door. A few moments later, a tall girl with long, wavy dark hair walked out onto the front step. Her skin was tanned. She wore jeans and a black T-shirt.

"May I help you?" she asked.

Tank had faced down some of the most evil characters in the world. But now as he stood staring at Jenny Von Dorn, Tank could feel his legs turn to overcooked spaghetti. His heart beat fast. His face turned redder than a radish.

"Um . . . um . . . um," he stuttered, "are you Jenny Von Dorn, daughter of Rudolph Von Dorn, a captain in the US Navy?"

"Yes, I am," Jenny answered. "Who are you?"

"My name is Tank, and your father is in a lot of trouble."

¤

While Tank told Jenny the most incredible story she had ever heard, her father continued terrorizing the East Coast. He used the Destructo Beams aboard the *Harpoon* and the *Hurricane* to burn up seaside towns. Gadget, now in command of the *Hurricane*, laughed as he saw thousands flee from the burning towns.

Cyclops was also slowly figuring out how the Amulator worked. He used the device to bring down meteors from space. They crashed to Earth in a terrible frenzy.

Pi looked down on the destruction as her transportsphere drifted high above the United States. "Pi to headquarters! . . . Come in, Athena."

"This is HQ, Pi. What's going on?" Athena asked hurriedly.

"Von Dorn is destroying everything!" Pi said. "But I don't believe he's working alone. Has the navy found the *Hurricane*?"

"Negative," Athena answered. "Dr. Stein and Colonel Bragg believe Von Dorn stole the sub. It had the extra cloaking device."

"That's what I think, too," Pi said. "Have you heard from Gadget? I still haven't been able to communicate with him."

"Negative," Athena said grimly. "He hasn't checked in since his last transmission, and that was ages ago. I don't know where he is. I'm afraid something simply awful has happened to him. D-Day senses something is wrong, too."

"I agree," Pi said. "I think Von Dorn is using Gadget and the Amulator. You need to shut down the device. Override the access pads."

"Roger that," Athena said. "Overriding now."

Nothing happened. The Amulator, which was located in a secret cave, would not shut off.

"Blast," murmured Athena. She tried again to shut down the device, but it was useless.

"Pi!" she yelled. "Nothing's happening. I can't shut down the Amulator. Do you think Von Dorn has control of Gadget's access pad?"

"I do," Pi shot back. "Gadget must have shown him how to shut down the manual override."

"Why would Gadget show him how to use it?" Athena blared. "Von Dorn can do anything with that access pad!"

"I'm afraid Gadget is working with Von Dorn," Pi said, her voice trailing off in despair.

"Gadget wouldn't do that unless he was forced. We're doomed," Athena said forlornly.

It wasn't far from the truth.

¤

"I don't know who you are, or why you're telling me these awful stories about my dad. Leave right now or I'm calling the police."

"They won't come," Tank said to Jenny. "Colonel Bragg has seen to that. Listen, Jenny,

I know you don't know me, but what I am saying is the truth. I can prove it to you."

"How?" Jenny asked.

Tank tapped the access pad on his wrist.

"See this device? I can push this button and in a split second it will transport us to Kid Squad headquarters. All your questions will be answered there. We need your help. The world needs your help."

Jenny stared at the access pad locked on Tank's wrist.

"I don't believe you," she said.

"See for yourself."

Tank grabbed Jenny's hand and pressed the button on his access pad. In an instant, they were standing in the middle of Kid Squad headquarters.

"Wow!" Jenny yelled in wonder. "How did you do that?"

"Never mind," Tank said. "This is Athena, another member of the Kid Squad. Look at the monitor. It's the Oval Office in the White House."

"Is that the president and the vice president?" Jenny asked.

"Sure is," Athena blurted. "They're waiting to talk to Captain Cyclops . . . your father."

"Captain Cyclops?" Jenny asked.

"That's what your dad calls himself," Tank responded, "ever since the accident."

The meeting began. Guest starring during the teleconference was the president's family, who sat with their mouths taped shut.

"Good afternoon, Mr. President and Mr. Vice President. My name is Captain Cyclops. You know me as Captain Rudolph Von Dorn, US Navy. I'm not going to waste your time going over recent events. Mr. President, you're well aware that I have your wife and daughter on board.

"As you know, I am in control of two nuclear-powered submarines, the *Harpoon* and the

Hurricane. Each is equipped with nuclear missiles, an Invisashield, and a Destructo Beam of my own making. You already know I have used some of these instruments. I also have in my control the Amulator, a dreadful weapon in the wrong hands."

The president seemed shocked.

"What do you want?" the vice president shouted.

"Jerome, dear boy, I don't want anything. I can have everything and anything I wish. My submarines will see to that. What I will do, however, is rain terror down on the world. Simple destruction. That's what I seek because it thrills me."

"You're mad!" the president shouted.

"As is my crew, Mr. President. We are a horrific accident of science. We will continue our path of devastation until we ourselves are destroyed, which I suspect will never happen.

The *Harpoon* and the *Hurricane* are marvels of military science even without the Invisashield.

"It is my plan to lay waste to towns, cities, islands, and countries. But first, I will drop off your family on a remote island. Then I will destroy it while you watch helplessly from the White House. Catch me if you can, Mr. President, but I don't think you will."

The transmission abruptly ended.

Jenny, standing at Kid Squad headquarters, thought of the grotesque image of her father. The president of the United States, sitting at his desk, thought of his family, trapped and at the mercy of the evil captain. He doubted he would see them again. Jenny and the president began sobbing.

Chapter 8
"You're Fired!"

"Pi, this is Gadget. Come in. . . . Come in."

Flying high in the transportsphere, Pi was more than excited to hear Gadget's voice crackle over the radio.

"Gad, OMG, where are you? Are you okay?" Pi asked.

"Yes, of course. I'm fine. Cyclops hypnotized me with that dork burger eye of his. Then he took control of the Amulator. He forced me to tell him how to override the manual shutdown. Sorry about that. I really had no say in the matter.

"Still, I came out of it and was able to escape. I'm on the *Hurricane* now. The crew abandoned her yesterday. The cloaking device was malfunctioning, so they all returned to the *Harpoon*. Can you get a fix on my location?"

"Roger, locking on to you as we speak," Pi responded. "Are you hurt?"

"Negative," said Gadget. "I figure we can use the *Hurricane* to stop Cyclops and regain control of the access pad. I have a plan. Contact the rest of the squad. Have them transport themselves to my location."

"I will," Pi said. "I'll see you soon. I'm glad you're all right."

"Roger," Gadget said. "I'll see you soon. Gadget signing out."

Gadget looked around the *Hurricane*'s control room. He smiled the most lying of smiles. "How did I do, captain?" he asked.

Cyclops trained his menacing eye on Gadget,

nodding in approval. "You did fine, Commander Gadget, just fine. Once we have your friends aboard, we can dispose of them and continue on our way. Then there will be nothing to stop us."

"Aye, aye, captain," Gadget bellowed. "I am at your service."

¤

"Mr. President, get ahold of yourself," Vice President Hershey barked. "It's time to fight fire with fire. General Marsh has a plan that will blow Cyclops to the other side of the moon."

The president, sad and mournful, wiped the tears streaming from his eyes on the cuff of his suit jacket. He couldn't get past the thought of losing his daughter and wife.

As he pushed away the last few tears, Colonel Bragg and Dr. Stein watched General Marcia Marsh rise from her seat. She briskly walked to the president's desk. Like a good soldier, the general stood at attention and waited for permission to speak.

"At ease, general," the president softly said. "What do you propose to do?"

Marsh, still stiff as a board, glanced over to the vice president, who nodded his approval.

"Mr. President, sir," the general began, "Colonel Bragg's Special Projects Division has bungled this operation from the beginning. They are no closer to stopping Captain Cyclops than they were when this situation began.

"Sir, I believe that we can sink the *Harpoon* and the *Hurricane* and stop Captain Cyclops when he uses the Destructo Beam."

Bragg, who had been sitting silent, could no longer remain so. He bolted from his chair.

"That's all well and good, general," Bragg bellowed, "but we don't know when he's going to use the beam. We don't know where he is."

Marsh looked at the vice president, who again nodded.

"That's not entirely true, sir," Marsh said. "You heard him say he plans to put your wife and daughter on an island and then destroy it."

The general cleared her throat.

"Sir, once he destroys that island we will know instantly where Cyclops and the submarines are. Mr. President, sir, we can then fire several nuclear warheads at that location. That will destroy Cyclops and the subs for good. Anything swimming within 300 miles will be wiped out."

The president looked squarely at General Marsh. His once boyish face had grown much older in recent days. Worry lines burrowed deep into his forehead. His hair was grayer.

"*Unglaublich,* unbelievable," Dr. Stein said.

"Let me get this straight, general. You want to use my family as bait for your trap. And once

Cyclops kills them, you want to devastate the area with nuclear warheads? Is that what I'm hearing? Is that what you want to do?"

The general squirmed at the president's questions. She was just about to say something when the vice president spoke.

"What choice do we have, Mr. President?" the vice president said. "There's no other way of knowing where Cyclops is. By raining a nuclear storm down on his head, we can destroy him, the submarines, and all of the weapons he has on board. We'd be saving thousands, perhaps millions, of lives, sir. Surely you realize that."

The president slunk down in his seat and contemplated the consequences.

"Dog-blasted, this is madness, Mr. President," Bragg bellowed. "We'll find Cyclops, sir. Give us a chance. We won't set off a single nuclear bomb to do it."

Hershey looked at Bragg with daggers in his eyes. "You've already had your chance. You failed, colonel. General Marsh's plan will work.

"I'm sorry, Mr. President, that we have to sacrifice your family," the vice president continued, "but it's the only way. If we don't do what the general is asking us to do, Cyclops will terrorize the world. There will be no end to the destruction and to his madness. We can have nuclear missiles from three submarines and several stealth bombers hit the site within seconds of the island being blasted. He won't get away. Not with that much firepower."

The president didn't say a word. He knew the vice president was correct. If there was another way out of this mess, he didn't see it.

"It seems I am out of options," the president said sadly.

"Dog-blasted, Mr. President!" Bragg shouted. "You can't allow that to happen. Never mind what would happen to your family during this crazy scheme. Nuclear weapons will devastate the ocean, sir, for thousands of miles. It will foul the air as the wind blows radioactivity to Timbuktu and beyond. There's a better way. My kids will find Cyclops."

"Mr. President," Dr. Stein said, "there might be another way out of zee mess."

"Go on, doctor," the president said.

"I believe that for zee *Harpoon* to use zee Destructo Beam, or its Invisible Ray for that matter, zee ship has to, how you say, *materialize* for all to see," Dr. Stein said.

"I believe it can't fire zee weapon while it is invisible," he continued. "Witnesses have, how you say, *reported*, ah, yes, reported seeing a large whale before seeing a flash of bright light. That light, Mr. President, I believe is zee Destructo Beam and zee whale is zee *Harpoon*."

"Is that possible?" the president asked.

"It is," Dr. Stein said. "I have been working on zee calculation."

"The ship must have to materialize when it uses its weapons," Bragg said. "We can use this information to spring a trap and force the subs to the surface."

The vice president paused for a moment. He thought about what Dr. Stein had just said.

"Mr. President, the ocean is too vast. Even from the International Space Station we wouldn't be able to see a submarine in the time it takes for the *Harpoon* to materialize and fire the Destructo Beam. The only way is to allow Cyclops to obliterate the island. Then we will know where he is and where to aim our weapons. There's no other way, sir. No other way."

The president hesitated. He thought about what Dr. Stein had said. He thought about his family. Tears again streamed down his face. His daughter was so young, only sixteen. Sacrificing her was too much for a country to ask.

"What am I to do?" he asked, mostly to himself.

"Mr. President, the decision is yours," the vice president said. "You know where I stand."

"I don't know what I should do," said the president sorrowfully. "All I can think about is my family, not the country. Jerome, help me."

The vice president was ready for this moment. He gladly seized the opportunity.

"Mr. President, it's obvious that you are in no position to carry out your duties as commander in chief," the vice president said. "The fate of your family, sir, has clouded your judgment.

"As you know, the US Constitution's Twenty-fifth Amendment allows the president to voluntarily hand over authority to the vice president or the person next in the line of succession when he is unable to perform his duties. I suggest, sir, that you do so immediately."

The president nodded. He got up and walked to the large window behind his desk. He looked out on the White House lawn. Workers were busily raking leaves on this glorious autumn day. Two men in overalls joked with one another as a squirrel ran across the lawn.

"You're right, Jerome," the president said quietly. "I'm putting my family in front of the nation. I'll sign a letter temporarily giving you authority until such time as this crisis is over."

"No, Mr. President," Bragg screeched. "Give us a chance to find Cyclops first. We can do it. We dog-blasted can."

No one heeded Bragg's pleas.

A few minutes later, the deed was done. The president signed the letter giving Vice President Jerome Hershey the power to make decisions. The president left the Oval Office, his head lowered, his eyes staring blankly at the carpet as he walked.

"General Marsh, put your plan into action," the vice president ordered. "Colonel Bragg, have your forces and the Kid Squad stand down."

"You can't, Mr. Vice President," Bragg protested. "You can't. Marsh's plan is a fool's errand. It will surely kill the president's family, devastate the environment, and not succeed in destroying Cyclops. That submarine can dive faster than a seagull on a dish of half-eaten French fries. You need to reconsider."

"The order is given, colonel," the vice president responded. "You're fired."

Chapter 9
Reunion

"Gad, old boy, good to see ya." Tank was truly happy to see his friend. He let Gadget know it with a hearty slap on the back. *Jeez, I wish he wouldn't do that*, Gadget thought. *It stings. It always stings.*

Tank, Athena, Pi, and Jenny had used the Amulator to teleport themselves to the *Hurricane.*

"We were awfully worried about you. This here is Jenny, Captain Von Dorn's daughter. She's going to try to talk some sense into her father."

"I'm glad to see you too, Gad," Pi said.

"So am I," Athena added. "D-Day is too, although I left him back at headquarters. He saw you on the visorscreen and knew immediately something was wrong. He's such a smart kitty."

"Dr. Stein says there's a good chance that if Cyclops gives up soon, the Amulator can reverse the effects of the cloaking device that caused everyone aboard the *Harpoon* to go bonkers," Tank added, twirling his finger in the air. "He has to wave the white flag soon, though, or the effects will be irreversible."

Gadget walked around the *Hurricane*'s control room. He looked at each one of his friends. He knew who they were, but he felt no love or kinship with them.

"So, Gad, old buddy, Pi says you have a plan," Tank said. "Care to share? Not everyone has a real submarine he can play with. Officially we're not even on the case. Colonel Bragg pulled us off. But we're not listening to him today."

"Yes, we're disobeying orders," Pi said. "What do you have in mind?"

Gadget stopped pacing and stared. "Well, there's been a change in plans," he said, wiping his glasses clean with his shirt.

Suddenly, several of the crew members, their bodies ravaged by decay, stormed into the control room. They took each member of the Kid Squad and Jenny prisoner. They then seized each of the access pads.

"Gad, what's gotten into you?" Tank barked. He was more than mad.

"I'm sorry, but there's no other way," Gadget said. "The captain and I couldn't let you ruin our tour of destruction, so I had to lure you into a trap. Don't worry, though. I'll make sure your deaths are quick. The captain promised they would be."

"Gad, have you gone crazy?" Athena shouted.

"He's not crazy," Pi said. "He's still under Cyclops's hypnotic spell."

"Yes, yes he is," Cyclops said, walking into the control room. Everyone gasped. "With you out of the way, we can continue on our journey."

"Dad?" Jenny screamed.

Although Jenny was revolted by his appearance, the man with one eye was still her father. The eye glared at her. His face was sickly yellow. The whole crew, besides Gadget, looked like the creatures in the horror movies Jenny had seen against her mother's wishes.

"Who is this young lady?" Captain Cyclops asked, not recognizing his own daughter.

"Dad, it's me, Jenny, your daughter. Don't you know who I am?"

The captain's eye looked the girl over again.

"I'm sorry, young lady. I don't know who you are," he said. He quickly got back to the work at hand. "Things have changed, Commander Gadget.

We're going fishing, and we're going to use the Kid Squad as bait. Have you ever seen a great white shark up close? Not to worry. You will."

Cyclops walked over to a chart spread on one of the tables in the control room. He motioned for Gadget to come over. The captain then planted a finger squarely on a small island.

"Commander Gadget, the ship is yours," Cyclops roared. "I will be aboard the *Harpoon*. After you dispose of your friends, we will meet at this tiny island at 1500 hours. We'll maroon the president's family. Then we'll use the Destructo Beam to blow the place to bits. They'll be able to see the explosion from space."

"Aye, aye, captain," Gadget said. "I am at your service."

¤

"When I get Gadget home, I'm going to wring his scrawny little neck," Tank said. He paced around the submarine's tiny prison.

"What a dork burger," Athena added. "How could he turn on his only friends? He's a traitor. I'm never speaking to Gadget again as long as I live."

"No," Pi said. "Gadget is under the spell of Cyclops. We have to figure out a way to break that spell."

"Tank, I'm scared," Jenny whispered.

"Don't worry, Jenny, we've gotten out of tighter jams than this."

Tank was lying. This was the tightest jam ever.

"I know he's your dad and all that, but I'd like to punch that bag of puss in the eye," Tank said. "Did you smell that control room? Pew! All those ghouls are turning into onion jelly."

"Yuck, onion jelly?" Athena said. "That sounds awful. I bet it tastes awful, too. My nana makes a nice raspberry jelly. I hope I get to eat it again."

"He's not my dad, not anymore," Jenny said, ignoring Athena's ramble down memory lane. "I don't know what he is, or who he is."

"It's not his fault," Athena reminded Jenny. "That cloaking device, or whatever that thingamabob is called, malfunctioned. It was an accident."

Tank looked at Pi, his expression serious. The Kid Squad was in danger. Tank knew it. Pi knew it. Everyone in the brig knew it. Gadget was going to make them walk the plank.

"What's your plan, Pi?" Tank asked.

"I don't know if it will work, but it's worth a try," Pi said. "I read once that when a person hypnotizes another person, it's like the hypnotist opens a control panel in that person's brain and reprograms their mind."

"I think I know what you mean," Athena said. "Once, my uncle Gary went to a hypnotist to help him lose weight. The hypnotist told my uncle that every time he reached for a piece of pie, he'd have enough willpower not to eat it. Of course, it didn't hurt that my aunt is a lousy cook. Maybe that's the real reason my uncle lost fifty pounds."

"Anyway," Pi continued, "if we can open the control panel in Gadget's brain again, maybe we can deprogram him."

"How do we do that?" Athena asked.

Pi shrugged her shoulders.

¤

With Gadget in command, the *Hurricane* sliced through the water, invisible and fast. The *Harpoon* was nearing the island on which Cyclops was going to maroon the president's family and then blow them to bits. Once the deed was done, he planned to destroy every coastal city in the world, and maybe launch a few nuclear missiles inland.

"Commander Gadget, we're nearing the feeding grounds of the great whites," said the

Hurricane's helmsman. Her bloody, green hands skillfully maneuvered the submarine. "What are your orders?"

"Surface and bring the prisoners up top," Gadget responded. "Make sure they're shackled."

The strange, goblin-like crew of the *Hurricane*, who had set sail just days before on the *Harpoon* as able-bodied sailors, did as instructed.

The sun beat down on the wet deck of the submarine, where Tank, Pi, Athena, and Jenny stood. They all felt the warm sea air blow against their faces. It made Pi guess the submarine was nearing the Caribbean Sea. Their hands were cuffed in metal shackles. A member of the *Hurricane*'s crew poured chunks of red, bloody meat into the water. Everyone waited for the sharks to take the bait.

"Gad, think for a second," Pi began. She hoped to open the "control panel" in his brain. "We're friends. We've been friends since first grade. I'm your friend. Tank is your friend, and so is Athena. Cyclops brainwashed you with that evil eye of his. You have to fight it. You have to remember."

"Yeah, old buddy," Tank said. "Don't be a dork burger and make us sleep with the fishes. Speaking of fishes, remember the time we put that spoiled cod in Craig Lumpersickle's locker after he took Little Pauli's lunch money? Holy guacamole, he couldn't get the smell out for weeks. His locker smelled worse than old Mr. Morrison's socks. Ms. Dombrowski kept us after school for a week, but it was worth it."

Gadget peered across the open water not saying a word.

Craig Lumpersickle was a jerk. No one at Copernicus Middle School would say otherwise. But after Gadget and Tank had put the stinky fish in his locker, Craig never bothered anyone again.

"Remember when you helped me with my science project?" Athena said. "OMG, that remote control volcano you helped me make blew its top like nobody's business. I don't know what you put inside that thing, but when it exploded, it covered the Gossip Gals in orange goo. That gave those chatterboxes something to talk about. I got an A-plus, all thanks to you, Gadget."

A slight smile crossed Gadget's face. He remembered.

Not far away, the dorsal fins of four great white sharks sliced through the water. They sensed the bloody chum. When they arrived, they would be pleasantly surprised to find out what was really on the menu.

"How about the great time we had at the Shake & Stir two weeks ago to celebrate your birthday?" Pi asked. "Sally Whitenhouse was there. She told me she likes you, but I promised I wouldn't say anything. We all know you like her too."

Then the sharks swarmed.

Chapter 10

The Best Laid Plans

Twelve of the US Air Force's most sophisticated bombers circled high over the Atlantic. Their nuclear-tipped missiles were ready to wing their way into battle. Three attack submarines also made their way into position. Their nuclear cargo was also armed and ready.

No one knew which island Cyclops planned to destroy. However, keeping watch overhead were fleets of spy satellites, radar planes, and the International Space Station itself. Once the island was gone, the nuclear armada would target the blast area and launch its atomic cargo.

"Nothing within 300 miles of the island can survive the force of the impact," General Marsh told Vice President Hershey as they monitored the status inside the White House Situation Room. President Novak was upstairs in his study. He could not bear to watch his family die.

"Are you sure the *Harpoon* and the *Hurricane* cannot escape?" the vice president asked. "If they do, we'll be in a bigger mess than we are in now."

"There's always a possibility that the subs can escape," Marsh said.

"Let's hope they don't, Marsh," Hershey said. "For your sake and my sake, let's hope they don't."

¤

"*Harpoon* to *Hurricane* . . . come in, over," Lieutenant Spider radioed.

"This is *Hurricane*," Gadget announced. "Over."

"The captain wants to know whether you will arrive at the island as scheduled, over."

"Roger that," Gadget answered.

"Good. He also wants to know whether you have taken care of the prisoners, over."

"Roger that," Gadget said. "There's nothing left of them. The sharks seemed pleased."

"Copy that," Spider said. "*Harpoon* out."

Gadget looked at Tank, Pi, Athena, and Jenny. He grinned. "I hope you guys know how to sail a nuclear submarine," he said.

Gadget was Gadget once again. Friendship was too strong. It broke the hypnotic hold Captain Cyclops had on him. Now it was time to stop the evil captain before he could hurt anyone else.

"So tell me again what we're going to do," Tank said.

"For one thing," said Pi, "Gadget is going to hook up the Amulator to the Destructo Ray. Once we're in range of the *Hurricane,* we're going to zap it with the world's largest Freeze Ray and turn it into the biggest ice cube ever."

"It shouldn't be too hard to do," Gadget said. "I'll bypass the electromagnetic fluctuation sensor . . . "

"Whoa . . . whoa . . . ," Tank interrupted. "Just give me the headlines, not the entire story."

"Once the *Hurricane* is incapacitated," Pi said, "Tank and I will board the submarine and take it over. We'll then teleport Cyclops and the crew to Bragg's headquarters. There, Dr. Stein will work to reverse the effects of the radiation. Hopefully, everyone will be all right."

"Meanwhile, I'll rescue the president's wife and daughter," said Athena. "I'll use the Amulator to teleport them back to the White House."

"Sounds simple enough," Tank said.

Plans that sound "simple enough" often become more complicated, Gadget thought.

¤

The wind was calm on the deserted island. Cyclops and several members of his crew stood on the white beach. They watched the First Lady and her teenage daughter crawl over the sand.

"You'll never get away with this," Mrs. Novak said. "They'll hunt you down like the animal you are."

"I totally expect that, Mrs. Novak," Cyclops responded. His one eye glared at the First Lady, who was now tightly hugging her daughter. "And if I shall perish, as I certainly expect to, I will die knowing that you two are gone. I will also have taken thousands of others with me.

"In the meantime, I will repair to my lair aboard the *Harpoon* and blast this tiny rock to the heavens. Once that is accomplished, the *Harpoon* and the *Hurricane* will devastate the world. Mrs. Novak, I bid you and your daughter adieu."

Cyclops returned to the *Harpoon*. He ordered the crew to stand by as Gadget and the *Hurricane* sped to meet them.

¤

Some 2,000 miles away from the president's wife and daughter sat another tiny island where no one lived. There were no animals on the island, not even a bird.

However, the island had one somewhat remarkable feature—a volcano. The volcano hadn't erupted for 400 years. Yet just thirty minutes after Cyclops returned to the *Harpoon*, the unexpected happened. The tiny volcano erupted in a rage of smoke, fire, and rock.

Thousands of trained military eyes watching radar and computer screens for Cyclops saw the explosion and assumed the worst. Also watching in disbelief was General Marsh and Vice President Hershey.

Marsh ordered her planes and submarines to fire their nuclear missiles at the location of the explosion. She believed Cyclops had kept good on his promise and had blown the island to pieces. Within moments, those missiles hit the island. The nuclear wind fanned out for hundreds of miles in each direction.

"We got Cyclops," the general cheered. "Nothing could survive that attack."

Of course, Cyclops did survive the attack. The *Harpoon* was nowhere near the target. The captain watched on the *Harpoon*'s computers as the unmistakable remains of a radioactive mushroom cloud billowed into the air.

Minutes later, Cyclops's angry yellow eye appeared on every computer and video screen in the White House Situation Room. Marsh and Hershey watched in wide-eyed horror.

"You insufferable fools!" Cyclops yelled. "You thought that volcanic eruption was the *Harpoon* destroying the island where I put the president's family? You thought you could carpet bomb the ocean and kill me? Ha! How stupid."

"Von Dorn!" yelled Marsh. "You need to surrender immediately."

"What will you do if I don't? Bomb another volcano into oblivion? You have no idea where I am. The president's family is safe for now. I'll deal with them later. I'm plotting a course to Washington DC so I can fire my own nuclear missile. In fact, General Marsh, I'm going to use your office as my target."

He cut off the transmission. Then he radioed Gadget aboard the *Hurricane* to meet him at another point on the map.

"We're going to light a firecracker under General Marsh and Vice President Hershey," the captain barked.

Gadget looked at Pi, who looked at Tank, who looked at Athena.

"What's our plan now?" Tank asked Pi.

"Same as it was before," Pi responded. "The president's family is safe, but Washington isn't."

Gadget interrupted. "There is one problem," he said. "I can't bypass the electromagnetic fluctuation sensor without blowing up the ship. No matter what I do, I can't get the Amulator to access the cloaking device. It seems Von Dorn designed the cloaking device to destroy itself if an enemy tried to tinker with it."

"So what now?" Tank asked.

Pi thought for a second. "We'll have to do it the old-fashioned way. We'll meet as he asked. We'll disable the ship with one of the *Hurricane*'s torpedoes. Then we'll board the *Harpoon* like pirates. We'll battle the crew on board. Our access pads are juiced and we're ready to roll."

"Ahoy, matey," Tank said, mimicking a pirate. "Me likes them odds. Shiver me timbers and yo, ho, ho."

Jenny cracked a smile. Athena giggled. Pi rolled her eyes.

"You're such a dork burger," Gadget said, laughing.

Chapter 11
Battle Stations!

The battle began. It was a surprise to Cyclops. He thought Gadget was still his ally. "Soon we will be an unstoppable armada," the captain had said earlier to Spider. "We will wreak havoc across the seven seas."

"Captain!" Sully yelled. "Torpedo off the starboard side. Sir, I don't know where it's coming from. There are no ships in the vicinity. Sir, I think the *Hurricane* is firing on us."

Cyclops couldn't believe what he had just heard. "This is mutiny!" he yelled. "Spider, hard to port, full speed ahead."

"Aye, aye, captain," Spider acknowledged.

"He's let go another one, sir," Sully yelled. "And another. Three incoming."

"Confound it!" Cyclops exclaimed. "Even though we're invisible, that boy knows what our position is. He knows where I am, but I can't see him. Can you get a fix on his position?"

"Negative," Sully responded.

"What are your orders?" Spider asked.

"Dive to 1,000 feet . . . ," the captain ordered.

The ship rocked violently as one of the torpedoes exploded above. Another tossed about sailors, dishes, maps, and chairs. Cyclops grabbed a table and held tight as the ship listed.

"That little brat is trying to force us to the surface!" Cyclops yelled. "He's exploding the torpedoes in a pattern. That kid is smart."

"Sir, two more torpedoes coming at us," Sully cursed.

Blam, blam! The explosives rocked the *Harpoon* one after another. Water poured into the control room. One crew member, his arms and legs ravaged by radiation, struggled to turn a big screw and close the leak. Several sailors had smacked their heads against the side of ship.

"Any idea where he is, Sully?" Cyclops asked.

"Negative, sir. Judging from the position the torpedoes came from, he's somewhere in front of us. Although I don't know how far away he is."

"Forward torpedo room," Cyclops ordered, "fire all torpedoes in a wide pattern. Keep firing until I give you the order to stop. Set their fuses for medium range."

"Aye, aye, captain," came a voice from the torpedo room.

"Three more torpedoes coming straight for us," Sully warned.

"Dive, Spider, dive!" the captain yelled as yellow puss oozed from his eye.

"Can't, captain," Spider shot back. "That last explosion damaged our dive control. We need to surface fast or we will be stuck here forever."

"Sir," Sully barked, "torpedoes 1,000 yards away and closing fast."

"Did our torpedoes hit anything?" Cyclops asked.

"Not that I can tell," Sully said. "They're 600 yards and closing . . . 500 yards . . . 400 yards . . ."

Rudolph Von Dorn was one of the navy's best submariners. Now he, as Captain Cyclops, froze in the heat of battle. He didn't know what to do. All he could hear was Sully's bark. "Now they're 300 yards . . . 200 yards . . ."

The pressure was too great.

Spider kept urging Cyclops to surface. "If we surface, he'll surface. Then we can fire the Destructo Beam in a wide arc. We can blast that little brat and his friends to pieces even if they are invisible."

Spider was right. "Surface . . . surface," the captain bellowed. Just then, a torpedo rammed into the side of his sub.

"I think that one got her," Pi said. "It's hard to tell. The *Harpoon* is still invisible. Let's surface. He still can't see us."

"Aye, aye, captain," Gadget said.

Gadget brought the *Hurricane* to the surface. He used the submarine's cameras and other detection gear to scan the sea for any trace of the *Harpoon*.

"She's out there, I know it," Gadget said.

Tank and Athena raced from the torpedo room to the control room.

"How's that for shootin'?" Tank asked.

"Nice job, you dork burger," Gadget said. "Now, let's see if Cyclops has surfaced."

Everyone climbed up to the deck of the submarine. They were confident the *Harpoon* was injured, but it was still invisible.

When they reached topside, the faint outline of the *Harpoon* appeared. It was hazy at first.

But soon everyone could see the shape of the sub.

"Over there!" Athena yelled, pointing to her right.

"He's getting ready to fire," Pi said.

"Holy guacamole!" exclaimed Gadget. "Everyone, adjust your access pads to create a protective shield around the *Hurricane*. Hold on tight and keep your fingers crossed. The Destructo Beam is powerful."

The members of the Kid Squad adjusted their access pads. They wrapped a protective blanket of energy around the *Hurricane*.

A bright blue light flashed in front of them. The kids shielded their eyes. They did as Gadget suggested and crossed their fingers.

¤

"Direct hit, sir," Spider yelled. "But, but . . . they're still afloat. I don't understand it. They should have been blown to Mars."

"They saw us," said Cyclops. "The beam takes up too much energy. I was afraid of that. They used the Amulator to create a shield. I should never have given back Gadget's access pad."

"So, all of our weapons are useless?" Spider asked.

"I'm afraid so, my old friend," Cyclops said. "The *Harpoon* is badly damaged. We can't set sail. Our weapons are useless. And each of us is slowly dying. They won't take us alive, however. Have the crew rig one of the nuclear missiles to go off aboard the ship. I suspect their Amulator can't protect them from a point-blank nuclear blast."

Just then a soft voice crackled over the radio.

"Dad, it's Jenny. . . . Do you remember me?"

Tears welled up in the captain's eye. Cyclops, Von Dorn in another life, then remembered his daughter, Jenny. *That girl . . . that girl on the* Hurricane. *That's my daughter . . . that's my daughter, Jenny. Jenny the Penny, I used to call her when she was a baby.*

"Dad, my friends talked to Dr. Stein," Jenny continued. "He knows there was an accident that made everyone aboard sick. He says he can help you and your crew. But you need to surrender now or it will be too late. Dad . . . Dad, can you hear me?"

All was quiet for a moment. The only sound was the gentle lapping of ocean waves on the hull of the *Harpoon.*

"Jenny, this is your pop. This is your dad," Cyclops said. His voice sounded rough, like sandpaper. "I love you very much, sweetheart, and I'm sorry for all this. I hope you can forgive me."

He shut off the radio.

"Spider, tell the crew to abandon ship. Tell them thank you for their loyalty. Tell them that they were the best crew a sub commander could ever have."

"What about you, captain?" Spider asked.

"A good captain always goes down with his ship."

¤

The auditorium at Copernicus Middle School was empty as Gadget sat on the stage playing his cello. It was a sad song, which matched Gadget's mood.

Tank stood in the shadows and listened as his friend played. He slowly walked up to the stage and sat down.

"Why so glum, chum?" Tank asked.

Gadget stopped playing and cradled the cello. He looked out into the auditorium's darkness.

"I let you guys down," he said. "I almost got you killed."

"Hey, old buddy, no biggie," Tank said. "Could have happened to any one of us."

"But it didn't," Gadget said. "It happened to me. I failed my friends, and I failed the Kid Squad. You'd be fish food if you hadn't knocked some sense into my head with all those sappy stories."

"It all worked out in the end, dude," Tank said. "We saved the world, yet again, and Dr. Stein is helping all the crew members of the *Harpoon*.

"All those ships that disappeared, including that carrier group, are all safe and sound thanks to you. Your idea of using the Amulator to reverse the Invisible Ray was genius, once you figured out how to bypass the whatchamacallit without blowing us up into little pieces."

"The electromagnetic fluctuation sensor," Gadget added.

"Yeah, that thing," Tank said. "All we did was go to their last positions and presto, everyone materialized like a magic trick."

"Yeah, that was pretty smart of me," Gadget said.

"Not only that," Tank continued, "President Novak gave Dr. Stein and Colonel Bragg their jobs back. Hershey resigned. Marsh is cleaning latrines. And the First Family is having dinner as we speak. And I even got to take Jenny out for a burger at the Shake & Stir before she went back home. All's well that ends well, as that guy Shakespeare used to say."

Gadget smiled. Tank quoting Shakespeare. What next?

"So don't worry. You've done your job as you always do. Heck, even Cyclops, excuse me, Von Dorn, is back on dry land. Although he's still a couple burgers short of a barbecue, Dr. Stein says he'll be 'right as zee rain' one day, whatever that means. He won't even have a droopy eye anymore. Isn't science wonderful?"

"You're the one who saved his life," Gadget said. "If it wasn't for you, Von Dorn would have gone down with the *Harpoon* once we rescued his crew."

"'Twas, nothin'," Tank said with a slight grin. "I sort of figured he was going to be all dramatic. So I just used the Amulator to stop time while I climbed aboard the *Harpoon* before he hit the self-destruct button. I put the old guy in cuffs.

"Before he knew it, he was on Dr. Stein's operating table getting an extreme, and I mean *extreme*, makeover. I hope Dr. Stein can do something about that guy's smell."

"Still, I wish I could be more like you," Gadget said. "You wouldn't have turned on your friends. You're strong."

"Nonsense, Gad old boy. You're the strongest person I know . . . and the smartest. Now why don't you play me a tune on that big fiddle of yours?"